For my three stars and Baby Billy – *K.L.*

For John and Pamela – *J.L.*

Shine copyright © Frances Lincoln Limited 2002
Text copyright © Karen Langley 2002
Illustrations copyright © Jonathan Langley 2002

First published in Great Britain in 2002 by Frances Lincoln Limited
First American Edition

Marshall Cavendish
99 White Plains Road
Tarrytown, New York 10591

Library of Congress Cataloging-in-Publication Data
Langley, Karen. Shine! / by Karen and Jonathan Langley.
Summary: Jimmy practices "shining" for his role in the school Nativity play.
[1. Fathers-Fiction. 2. Stars-Fiction. 3. School plays-Fiction. 4. Christmas-Fiction.]
I. Langley, Jonathan, ill. II. Title. PZ7.L2664 Sh 2002 [E]-dc21 2002000887

ISBN 0-7614-5127-7

Printed in Singapore

1 3 5 6 4 2

SHINE

Karen and Jonathan Langley

MARSHALL CAVENDISH

"Dad! Dad! I'm a star in the school play," said Jimmy.
"I've got to shine. Will you come and see me?"

"You'll have to practice hard," said Dad.
"I will come and watch you, as long as I'm not called out."

Just then the telephone rang.

"Here we go again," said Dad. "Run upstairs and get ready for bed, and I'll come and say goodnight before I go."

Jimmy washed his face, cleaned his teeth, and brushed his hair.

"Am I shining, Dad?" said Jimmy.
"You're beginning to sparkle," said Dad.

Sometimes Dad worked at night when it was dark,

so Nana put Jimmy to bed.

Next day the play rehearsals began.
Every day the children practiced.

Every day Jimmy practiced shining.

"Am I shining, Dad?" asked Jimmy.
"Yes, you're glimmering tonight," said Dad.

"I hope you can come and see me, Dad,"
said Jimmy.

The day of the show came.
   "Will you come and see me, Dad?" asked Jimmy.

"I'll do my very best, Jimmy," said Dad, as he left
the house and went out into the darkness with his toolbox.
"It starts at 7 o'clock!" Jimmy shouted after him.

Jimmy went back to school after supper. It was very dark.
   "What's in the bag?" asked Nana.
   "Oh, just some stuff I need for the play," replied Jimmy.

There were lots of people in the hall at school.
Jimmy couldn't see his Dad.
'I hope Dad comes to see me shine,' he thought.

'I hope Dad comes to see me shine.'

'I hope he comes.'

'I'm sure he'll be here soon.'

'Where's my Dad?'

The play began.

The curtains swished.

The donkey bumped.

The sheep shoved.

The shepherds stumbled.

The angels giggled.

The kings sneezed.

Mary, Joseph and the baby Jesus snuggled.

It was nearly the end. Time for Jimmy the Star to travel across the stage and stand next to baby Jesus.

'Where's my Dad?' thought Jimmy, looking out into the audience.

Suddenly through the sea of faces Jimmy saw his Dad. His face seemed to be shining like a light out of the crowd, smiling at him.

Jimmy stood on his box holding the star up high

and he smiled and smiled and smiled.

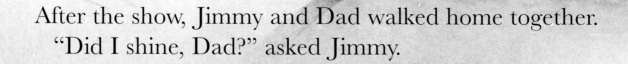

After the show, Jimmy and Dad walked home together.
"Did I shine, Dad?" asked Jimmy.

"You shone, Jimmy," said Dad. "You shone bright enough to light up even the darkest of skies."